Metaphorosis

January 2023

Beautifully made speculative fiction

Also from Metaphorosis

<u>Metaphorosis Magazine</u>

Metaphorosis: Best of 20xx
Metaphorosis 20xx: The Complete Stories
annual issues, from 2016

Monthly issues

<u>Plant Based Press</u>

Best Vegan Science Fiction & Fantasy
annual issues, 2016-2020

from B. Morris Allen:
Chambers of the Heart: speculative stories
Susurrus
Allenthology: Volume I
Tocsin: and other stories
Start with Stones: collected stories
Metaphorosis: a collection of stories

<u>Verdage</u>

Reading 5X5 x3: Changes
Reading 5X5 x2: Duets
Score – an SFF symphony
Reading 5X5: Readers' Edition
Reading 5X5: Writers' Edition

<u>Vestige</u>

The Nocturnals, by Mariah Montoya

Metaphorosis

January 2023

edited by
B. Morris Allen

ISSN: 2573-136X (online)
ISBN: 978-1-64076-249-7 (e-book)
ISBN: 978-1-64076-250-3 (paperback)

Metaphorosis
a magazine of speculative fiction
from
Metaphorosis Publishing

Neskowin

January 2023

Packing List for Oblivion

Cameron Bertron

The statue was nothing like Enefai remembered. Before, it had been buried to its stomach, with both hands reaching forward to rest almost perfectly, palms up, on the hungry earth. Age had softened the statue's face, which crawled with orange lichen, to a shroud. Its open mouth was turned up to the sky and overflowing with dust. Enefai had watched, for a long time, as the wind spilled grit from the corner of its lips like an hourglass. Now, suspended in holographic color in the center of the council chamber, it looked sanitized and frail. Enefai appraised it for the last time, knowing the outcome before the first votes flickered in. The piece was not particularly innovative; it was not of historic value. It was not vital, it was only beautiful. It would be left behind.

Enefai fixed her eyes on the statue as she cast her vote against it. No councilor volunteered to speak on the piece, so the judgement was swift. The holograph blinked and was replaced by a new sculpture, but the previous image stayed on in Enefai's mind. The decisions were getting harder. At its start, the council had been a mess of overdrawn debates and personal attacks. But Enefai would rather deal with the chaos of those early days than the current, brutal pace of their decisions. It had taken several years, but time had run out for ego and guilt. Enefai was reminded every moment, by the defeated silence of the council and the packing crates in her own home, that the world was ending this year.

The news had broken slowly, then all at once. Before the first dispatch shuddered their calm, Enefai's partner Moore had read the signs in the planet around her. For months, she had come home from the fields with her mouth twisted to one side, calloused fingers thrumming against her leg. She had tried to explain to Enefai about the sourness in the soil and the odd patterns of the rain. Enefai understood little beyond the alarm in her voice, but they both dared to hope that the change was peculiar to their region. It was not. The planet Kenlanli's terraformation was reversing. It had happened on a string of other planets. Now the societies of Kenlanli, so recently settled, were packing back up into the finite space of stations to await the terraformation of a new home planet.

Moore had volunteered immediately to work in the countryside, spending long months collecting soil samples to assess the rate of decay and assisting frontier families in their preparations to leave. The crisis had unwrapped something in her. She swung into action as though she had been preparing for it her whole life. Enefai had done her duty as well, accepting the summons to serve on the council for cultural preservation. She had also received requests for consent to send in her own collection for consideration. She left the requests to collect dust, with everything else in her studio.

Another sculpture was on display. Its superb craftsmanship was doomed by the choice of material. Marble was shipped in from off planet, and the piece would be judged insufficiently Kenlanliin. Enefai hoped that it would be taken in by another planet or station. In the far future, perhaps it could find its way back to Kenlanli's people wherever they might be. It was one of the few thoughts that still offered consolation.

The marble statue was the last of the day. When the session closed, Enefai brushed her way out of the chamber and through the honeycomb halls, exchanging a few nods and sympathetic words with her fellow councilors. Everyone's voice was low, their exchanges quick but sincere. They also had homes to pack. Enefai stepped outside to a sky bruised with evening and stretched her legs as she waded through the city's shallow outskirts into the countryside. The long path home took her past one of her own sculptures. She did not slow as she passed.

She had carved it the same year that she met Moore. As they rattled through the countryside in the back of a transport vehicle, Enefai had felt something tipping over inside her the longer she spoke with this sprawling woman in muddied boots. Probably it was the apocalypse playing tricks on her, but all the memories from that time felt warm. Enefai missed the weightless quiet between them. She missed the long evenings in her studio they spent tinkering at her worktable, Enefai with her designs and Moore with her tools or sketches. These days, the ice cracked beneath their every conversation. When Moore was not working in the countryside, she was brimming with hard choices. Enefai dodged conversations about the space station. She wanted to preserve at least the bubble of their home from the world outside as it ransacked itself. But Moore kept opening the door.

In her head, Moore was already living on the station. Sometimes, it even seemed to Enefai that she was excited about it. Moore planned ceaselessly, scrambling to assure Enefai that they would have everything they needed. But it wasn't their future that weighed heaviest on Enefai, even as it seemed to consume Moore, it was their life on Kenlanli. It was the slide of sand under her boots and the way that sunrise tangled in Moore's hair. In her birth province, at midday the desert's horizon disappeared with a shiver into the pale sky. How to forget that? How to remember?

Her back was slick with sweat when she saw the welcoming round roof of their home. As she stepped inside, the peace earned from her evening walk was dissipated by the boxes crowding the floor. Moore was out for the week, but due back any day. She had left Enefai a list of requests to help with the packing process. Enefai did not need to look at it. Everything was done except one item. She needed to pack her studio.

She quickly ate dinner and prepared a cup of tea. She kept herself moving, knowing that if she paused in her momentum, she would not do any packing tonight. Mechanically, she entered the studio and evaluated the single crate reserved for her belongings against the gentle mess of her studio. The floor and work benches were cluttered with models, sketches, and photos. Only her tools stood in perfect order, hanging on the walls and from the ceiling. The darkness outside converted the studio's large windows to mirrors and Enefai kept catching sight of her own movement as she worked. She tried to summon nostalgia as she packed, but her memories felt glossy and distant. Each tool slid into the crate only left her feeling heavier.

By the time she stopped for a break, her studio was decimated and her tea was cold. Enefai sat down heavily on the floor, her legs splayed in front of her and her back against a slab. Its porous rasp felt reassuring on the back of her arms. Years ago, she had brought the stone from her home province for a design she planned. The rock was unique to her home, stark white and ribboned with pale orange and crimson. As a kid, she used to find patterns in the traces of color, pulling shapes out of the cliffsides. She wondered bitterly what abstractions she would be able to find in the expressionless plaster they would use on station.

She slid away from the stone and regarded it from her place on the floor. She had seen more statues in the last few years than in all her life. She imagined their shapes in the slab and marveled at what had been accomplished with a piece of rock, a set of tools. But it hadn't saved them, extinguished in a flash of holographic light. With time, their craftsmanship, her craftsmanship, would be weathered back to featureless slabs like the one which stood before her. She felt powerless against that future, against her unreasoning anger at Moore's resilience, against her love for Kenlanli. She felt small beneath the slab that stretched above her. Hardening her gaze, she stared into the stone to calm her mind and began to slowly trace the fiery streaks in the rock from top to bottom.

She remembered the design she had planned for this slab when she picked it all those years ago. She could see now that it was all wrong. The arch of a spine was already in the slab's contour, thinly submerged. Veins of color netted together in the side. They would run over an open palm like sunlight. She could only catch the shape in pieces, barely coherent, but it was enough. The night hours were re-aligning. The studio's gravity bent around the work. Moore's expression when she inspected her crops, when she lifted a long shoot with the tip of her thumb, was already in the stone. Enefai reached for it. She smoothed the memorized lips and rounded the jaw. She crinkled the eyes that would watch, unflinching, as their planet's atmosphere slumped to reclaim the horizon. She followed only that instinct which had first searched out shapes in the mountainsides. She followed it until the sunrise dripped dirty pink into her studio.

When it was done, she would face it towards the window, pack her tools away, and leave this room forever. But for now, she closed her grainy eyes and pressed her forehead against the statue's unhewn base. Through her headphones she could not hear Moore's clattering entrance. The world was quiet as arms encircled her. Quiet as a kiss was buried on her neck. She would take it to the stars.

See Cameron Bertron's story "Packing List for Oblivion" online at Metaphorosis.
If you liked it, leave a comment. Authors love that!
Remember to subscribe to our e-mail updates so you'll know when new stories are posted.

About the story

This story was a way for me to explore climate anxiety. I had the conceit and setting for it before I had any of the characters. This was a problem when I started writing. I wanted the story to be character and relationship-driven, but I was caught up in the worldbuilding. I abandoned this story for almost a year. Then at the start of this summer, it came back to me. This time the characters and concluding scene were much clearer. I also wrote in the relationship between Moore and Enefai, which didn't exist when I started the story. Once I had the end scene visualized, I wrote toward it like a finish line.

A question for the author

Q: What is the hardest part about writing for you?

A: Usually, my stories start with a single image or emotion which I want to capture. After that image occurs, everything else is the hard part. Recently, what I've been finding the most difficult are scene transitions and set-up scenes. I know exactly what I'm about to say, but I can't set up the scene right to say it. Those set-up scenes take much more of my time than the climatic ones. The hardest part of writing will always change depending on the story and my skills as I acquire them. But for now, I'm wrestling with getting characters into the right place at the right time.

About the author

Cameron Bertron currently lives in Erdenet, Mongolia where she works as an English teacher. She has been a volunteer firefighter and a student of Slavic literature, but her most memorable work was as an almond milkman in her hometown Tampa, Florida.

The Knight Who Carried a Sword in His Heart

Joshua Hagy

Legends speak of a time when the world was different. For better or worse, it is impossible to tell, for none are alive who remember what was. All we have left of that time are dreams that were lived before they were written and the truths they hold for each of us.

Listen closely, for this is one such dream.

Thunderstorm rain pelted against the thick, oiled canvas of the tent as Lord

Philbreck closed his eyes and rested his head in his hands. He breathed deep, inhaling the summer scent of outside atop the musty odor tents never seem to lose no matter how often they are aired. The desk upon which he leaned and the chair in which he sat were both extravagances on a march, especially one as short as this, but they were touchstones of a sort, a comfort Philbreck refused to travel without. They were there for moments like this, when the weight of the past and the hope of the future were too much of a burden for one man to bear.

"Tomorrow," he said, the word barely audible over the late evening storm raging outside, "it will all be over." Philbreck sat with his thin arms drawn close, his back hunched over the table. He sat folded up, as if he were hiding for fear of the storm raging outside. He would stand in a moment, unfold himself into the tall man whose iron will took up more space than he ever would, but for now Philbreck protected something that he had not dared to feel in a very long time.

Hope.

"I pray it is so, my lord," said Abraham from the far corner of the tent. He sat upon a simple stool, wrapped in a philosopher's robes and marked with a philosopher's ink upon his forearms. The skin around his eyes was wrinkled with time, and his beard had moved beyond gray to the white only great age bestowed. His long, slender fingers looked as if they were made to hold the kind of thick book which now rested in his lap. They trailed along the edges, a silent wish that he could return to his reading rather than take up the thread of an argument he knew would not benefit either of them.

"Is that doubt I hear, Abraham?"

"It is faith, my lord."

"Faith." Philbreck laughed, but it was a gentle, teasing laugh. "You can't have faith without doubt. Otherwise, you'd know for certain, and you can't have faith in what you know for certain."

"Certainty breeds mistakes. You would do well not to be too certain of what you think you know and to be more certain of what you don't. A man could spend his entire life exploring the distance between those two points and count it well spent."

"I'll count my life well spent if no one ever has to lose their son the way I have," Philbreck said.

For all his learning, Abraham never quite knew what to say in these moments.

Silence wrapped itself around Abraham's heart. He wanted to speak, but even the right words, for all their power, wouldn't affect the young lord. Philbreck's father had listened to Abraham's advice. He had believed in magic and in the old ways that Abraham embodied and Philbreck was determined to set aside. Abraham had promised to look after Philbreck, but the young lord had long since turned away from his counsel. The old man remained with Philbreck more out of a sense of duty to his father than loyalty to the young lord who thought him a relic of bygone days.

The sounds of the storm intensified for a moment. Philbreck felt mist and wind for a brief moment before the sensation died away but gave it little thought. His men had finished setting camp just before the storm hit. It likely wouldn't last long, but it made campfires and a hot meal impossible. He figured most of them would climb into their tents and take advantage of the foul weather to catch up on their sleep. He wouldn't begrudge them that. They would need it tomorrow.

"My lord..." Abraham said.

"Yes?" Lord Philbreck looked up.

The man who stood before him lowered his cowl and looked first at Abraham and then at Philbreck, who stood and carefully placed his book upon his stool. He was not sure whom to address himself to, the elder who dressed like a philosopher of old or the man who was little more than a boy sitting at the table. "I am here to speak to Lord Philbreck," the newcomer said carefully, not wishing to offer disrespect so early in their meeting by making assumptions.

"Then speak," said Philbreck.

"I am the Knight Who Carries a Sword in His Heart," he said. He spoke his name like he was telling a story, and he hoped the weight of each word was enough for them to understand who he was. Abraham sat up straighter. "I've come to ask you not to slay the dragon."

Philbreck almost laughed. His first thought was the man was feverish and sick and needed help. His second, less charitable thought was that the man must have been mad to brave the thunderstorm, walk through a small army's camp, and barge into a lord's tent spouting nonsense.

But his third thought checked the first two. The man stood before him calmly, his eyes clear of all madness. He was bald. His face was bearded and strong, though lined with years. His cloak was simple. Beneath it he wore plain brown pants and a tunic befitting a peasant, not a knight. He was unarmed. There was no blade belted to his waist and there certainly wasn't one sticking through his heart. He looked like a scholar or a monk, but not a knight. There was nothing overtly threatening about him Philbreck could name, yet the tent felt smaller for his being there.

"Not slay the dragon," Philbreck repeated. "Why?"

"Because he is my friend."

Rain pattered against the tent. Thunder rumbled off in the distance. The storm was passing.

"A dragon is no one's friend," said Philbreck.

"He has witnessed ages and carries their wisdom. There are none left like him in the world. Byatt deserves to end his days peacefully. I'm asking you not to end greatness in bloodshed. Let him die in his own time. Please," the Knight's voice softened, "do not kill my friend."

The sincerity of the Knight's voice gave Philbreck pause, but only for a moment. He recognized pain when he saw it. He felt the Knight's pain echo in his own heart briefly before it reflexively hardened.

"He is a relic. The last in a long line of creatures holding us back from what we can be. They've ruled over us for centuries, but their time is over," said Philbreck.

"Byatt never claimed a kingdom. None of them did."

"They claimed our thoughts. Haunted our dreams. Made us fear the dark when we should have been carrying light into it. What could we have been? What could we have built without dragons binding our thoughts to superstition and magic?

"No," Philbreck shook his head. "It all ends tomorrow. Byatt's death will bring an end to the old ways. Take away the living talisman and all these misguided tales and superstitions will eventually go the way of legends, where they can do no harm."

Abraham spoke from the far corner of the tent. "My lord," he said gently. "This will not bring your son back. Nothing will."

"I know that." There was the echo in his heart again. Philbreck gritted his teeth against it. "But in a generation, maybe two, there will be minds free of magic and ghosts and old wives' tales and room for science and medicine. Someone will find a cure, so someone else's son won't have to die from a cough."

The Knight bowed his head. "I am sorry for your loss. I understand grief can be…"

"Do you have a child?" Philbreck cut him off.

"No."

"Then don't tell me you understand how it feels to watch your son cough his lungs up while the so-called wise men wave herbs in his face and burn sage and promise a cure they can't deliver because they've studied superstition instead of physic. Don't tell me you know what it feels like to lay your son in the cold ground. Don't tell me you know what it feels like to curse God with one breath and pray your son is safe in His arms with the next.

"I would have pulled every star down from heaven and drowned them, one by one, in the ocean if it would have meant he lived, but all I could do was watch him die. If killing a dragon means no one else has feel this, then so be it."

Outside, the rain stopped falling as the storm slid out of the full moon's path.

"I am sorry for your loss. I meant no disrespect. You are right. I cannot imagine what you must have gone through, but that doesn't change what I must do. I am the Knight Who Carries a Sword in His Heart. Byatt has long been my friend, and I name him thus. I will stand between him and all those who seek to do him harm."

"What exactly are you going to do about it?" Philbreck asked.

"If you pack up your army in the morning and leave, then we will part ways in peace. But if you and your men attack Byatt, I will draw my sword in defense of my friend and kill every one of you before I die."

"There are 200 of us," said Philbreck, scorn evident in his voice. His first suspicions had been right all along. The man was mad.

"Even so. I have been to The Dreaming Tree. I carry my purpose and your death in my heart."

"What the blazes are you talking about?"

"It is of the oldest tales, my lord," said Abraham. "Few know it now, but it is a tale that bears attention."

"That's exactly the kind of nonsense I'm talking about." Philbreck waved a dismissive hand in Abraham's direction. "You read a fairy tale and want to fight an army? Fine. Go ahead. But we will show you no mercy if you stand before us tomorrow."

"Nor I, you." The Knight spoke quietly, even regretfully. There was no bravado in the threat, only the certainty of man who saw a task to be completed before him.

He turned to leave.

"Sir Knight," said Abraham.

The Knight inclined his head and took note of Abraham's robes. "Philosopher," said the Knight.

Abraham keenly felt the burden of knowledge upon his heart in this moment.

"I know the old stories, and I know the tale of the Knight. Know that I am not your enemy."

"Then why are you helping him?" The Knight nodded in the direction of Philbreck, who glared his disapproval but did not give it voice.

"Because I treasure what he has lost."

The Knight considered this for a moment before he bowed to Abraham and left the tent.

The entrance to the dragon's mountain chamber was small and easy to overlook from the outside. It was barely wide enough for two men to walk abreast, and a tall man would need to duck. In stronger days, Byatt could shift into human form. When he had made the entrance, he kept it small. No one looked for dragons in tiny cracks.

The Knight found the torches where they had always been hidden, tucked into shadow just around the first bend in the tunnel. He spoke a word of magic, one borrowed from Byatt, and the torch came to life with a flame that gave off light, but not heat. The Knight took a deep, cleansing breath and felt time and weariness fall away from him.

He was home.

The path meandered only a little. The stone beneath his feet was level and the walls around him were smooth and dry. It was cool inside the mountain, but comfortably so, like the chill of blankets when you first slide beneath them.

As usual, Byatt smelled the Knight long before he entered the chamber.

"You smell of thunder." Byatt's voice was low and deep, but the power it once held had faded, like a receding tide reaching for a seaside cliff. "But you reek of Old Magic."

The Knight stepped from the tunnel and into Byatt's chamber. Torches on either side of the entrance bloomed to flickering life, giving him just enough light to see the dragon's face before him.

The Knight's heart was lifted by the familiar gruffness. "It's good to see you too, old friend." The Knight fought to keep his concern from showing in his voice. Only a few days had passed since he'd left Byatt, but the dragon looked as if he had aged further in that brief span. His once shimmering golden scales were grayed around the edges. The ones on his snout were entirely gray. As big as he was, Byatt looked smaller than he should, as if his insides had been hollowed slightly and he was settling in on his bones. Worse yet, the chamber was cooler than it should have been. Dragons were hot creatures by their very nature, but the fire inside Byatt had been banked down to embers buried beneath ash, unlikely to ever blaze to life again.

Byatt snorted. "I look old."

"You are old," said the Knight.

Byatt chuffed out a breath. "You found The Dreaming Tree. I can smell it on you."

The Knight stood before the dragon like a wayward son confessing his sins to a disappointed father. "I did."

Byatt sighed. "Why would you do this, when I asked you not to?"

The Knight lifted his gaze from the floor to meet the dragon's eye. "Because I've made a lot of wrong choices in my life. Let me make this right one."

Byatt closed his eyes in resignation. As much as he wished otherwise, there could be no going back. "I wish you hadn't done this."

"I know."

"Philbreck?"

"He's outside with 200 soldiers. They're coming for you in the morning."

"You should let them come. He isn't wrong in what he believes."

"Doing the wrong thing for the right reasons doesn't make it right," said the Knight. "But his son died. I think he lost himself a long time ago." The Knight shook his head. "I wish tomorrow didn't have to be."

"It doesn't," said Byatt. "My time is near anyway. Let me be. Let Philbreck have his way."

They both knew the Knight would not abandon his friend, but some words needed to be said for the comfort of having said them.

"We are who we are, my friend. There's nothing either of us can do about that."

"Then let tomorrow keep until morning," said Byatt. "Dark nights are better weathered with tall tales than quiet fears. Let's fill our hearts with something better than what awaits us tomorrow."

The Knight smiled. "What did you have in mind?"

"Would you read me a story?"

"Any story in particular?"

Byatt thought for a moment. There were many to choose from, but he realized there could only be one story for a night like this one. "How about," he said slowly, "the one that inspired you?"

The Knight looked into the darkness overhead. "If I'm going to read you a story, then I'm going to need more light."

Byatt's smile should have been terrifying, but the Knight found it comforting to know his friend could still smile. "I think I have enough magic left for that."

The dragon closed his eyes and took a deep breath. The torches extinguished themselves, casting the two of them into the true darkness that can only be found inside a mountain. The Knight held still, but kept his eyes turned upward. Slowly at first, moonlight soaked through stone and soil until it seeped into the cavern, filling it with the gentle light and soft shadows of summer's last full moon.

Above them, the chamber stretched to the mountain top, and its every wall was lined with stone shelves of books in neat rows. Ladders and walkways allowed access to every level in a maze of metal and stone.

Byatt's treasure had never been anything as cheap and pedestrian as gold.

"Can you find it?" Byatt asked. To the Knight's ears, he sounded more tired than he had a moment ago.

The Knight nodded. "I know exactly where it is." He'd been to the top of the library only once. There were more books here than a man could read in a lifetime, even if that was all he did with his life. But he knew the lower shelves well, and he could remember the exact location of every book he'd read. He'd spent many days here, and many nights reading to Byatt when the dragon was uninterested or, as of late, unable to shift forms to read for himself. The best books, like the one with the tale of The Knight Who Carried a

Sword in His Heart, echoed within him long after he finished reading them. He could remember exactly how it felt to sit with Byatt and be humbled by the sense of awe such tales poured into him. What must it have been like to take up the sword? What drove a man to such extremes?

Now he knew.

Unwilling to waste any of their precious time, the Knight jogged through moonlight to a ladder leading up to a second level shelf. He climbed it and two more before a short walkway led him to the slender, green volume that contained his favorite story. He held it up to show Byatt, but the dragon wasn't looking. He almost called out before he realized that Byatt wasn't focused on anything. He was waiting patiently, absently staring into moonlight's middle distance because eyes that once pinpointed mice from miles above the clouds could no longer see across their own chamber.

The sudden ache in the Knight's heart had nothing to do with the sword he carried there. He made his way back down the ladders, taking care to make as much noise as possible so Byatt could track him easily.

"Found it," said the Knight.

"Good." Byatt stretched his forelegs out before him. His hind legs did little more than shuffle as he tried to rise. Massive tendons creaked like ropes on a ship. Joints popped like cannon fire. Scales scraped against stone as he laid his head down upon his forelegs.

It was easy to imagine what Byatt had been, especially where moonlight erased the gray from his scales, but his face held onto the weary understanding that came at the end of a long life.

The Knight stepped around Byatt's paw and climbed into the crook of his elbow, where he could sit comfortably and lean against the dragon's head.

"Comfortable?" asked Byatt.

"Yes."

"Good."

The Knight willed time to slow down. Even better, to stop altogether. He wanted to preserve the perfection of this moment, when everything was quiet and still and he was home safe with his friend, reveling in the peace they'd stolen from the outside world.

But the moment was only perfect because they both knew it for what it was, and time had to pass for this to be true.

Life could only be lived in motion until it stopped, and they both knew this was an ending.

The Knight began to read. His voice cracked. He cleared his throat, wiped his eyes, and began again. Byatt closed his eyes and listened intently.

"Legends speak of a time when the world was different. For better or worse, it is impossible to tell, for none are alive who remember what was. All we have left of that time are dreams that were lived before they were written and the truths they hold for each of us. Listen closely, for this is one such dream."

It was a faerie tale, one of the first, about a neglected boy who grew up to become a solider who, being unfamiliar with kindness, angered his fellow soldiers until they left him to die on the battlefield.

"He cried out with his last breath, as all soldiers do, for anyone who could ease his pain or end it. It is said that in times of great desperation, or great need, The Dreaming Tree will hear us and answer our calls. The soldier's desperation was pure and his need grievous, so, in the space between final heartbeats, he found himself looking up at glimmering stars through the winter-bare branches of The

Dreaming Tree. He was in too much pain to speak, but The Dreaming Tree understood his need.

"The soldier awoke once more on the field of battle, carrying a sword in his heart. He knew it was powerful, and that it would allow him to defeat his enemies if he drew it, but the soldier knew he would die soon after his battle was finished. Rather than seek revenge, he took up the life of the knight errant. He wore no armor, and never again touched a bladed weapon. He travelled the land, lending strength and kindness where he found it lacking and, with each deed, the sword in his heart cut away a piece of the anger and hurt he carried.

"One night, as he looked up at winter's stars from his bedroll, he realized he had been his own greatest enemy. He found himself at The Dreaming Tree once again. He knelt before the tree, drew the sword from his heart, and lay down at the roots of the tree to rest at last."

The story at its end, the Knight closed the book quietly. Byatt's eyes remained shut. His breathing was shallower than it should have been. The old dragon was asleep beneath a blanket of moonlight, his body pressed hard against the cool stone floor of the chamber. It was hard for the Knight to imagine his sleep was restful, and harder still for him to see his friend reduced to such a hollow end.

Byatt's time was nearly over.

The Knight leaned his head against Byatt's. "Thank you for being my friend." Tears splashed against gray scales as the Knight wept silently. Byatt did not stir. The Knight was determined not to be angry at this end, though it was hard. Byatt deserved better, but there was no changing what was. There was only facing it.

Carefully, so as not to wake Byatt, the Knight clambered down from the dragon's embrace and left the chamber without speaking again.

They had lived their goodbyes. Let that be enough.

The Knight Who Carried a Sword in His Heart stood before the mountain and watched the sun rise for the last time. Patches of fog streamed along the valley below, pushed by a breeze so gentle it was almost nonexistent. He caught the barest hint of autumn's chill in the stillness of the morning. The Knight nodded, satisfied. He would not live to see the season come to pass. It was good that he could feel it, even if only in the slightest way.

The Knight waited. Armies, even small ones, take time to move. He could see the soldiers in the valley below, stirring about as they ate breakfast and readied weapons. The Knight could have walked down to their camp, but he was content to wait. Every passing moment was a moment stolen from death, and it was a beautiful day.

It was still early in the morning when the army formed ranks and marched in his direction. There were three men at the front, carrying banners. The Knight assumed Philbreck was the one in the middle, framed by his colors and bearing only the sword at his waist. The soldiers marched in orderly ranks behind the colors, save for one lone figure who followed behind the column. The Knight didn't have to see the figure's robes to know it would be Abraham who marched alone.

In time, the army reached the mountain. It was indeed Philbreck who rode between the colors, and he gave the order to halt. He stepped forward with the bannermen while the rest of his army waited within earshot. Philbreck wanted to make sure they heard what passed between the Knight and himself.

"Sir Knight."

"Lord Philbreck." He looked tall this morning. He was confident in who he was and what he was about, and he wore this confidence like armor. He believed in what he was doing. That made him dangerous.

The Knight did not quail before Philbreck and his army, for he believed, too.

"I told you last night there would be no quarter," Philbreck said. "This is your last warning. Stand aside. Let us pass, and we will part ways in peace. But know if you raise a hand against me or my men, you will be cut down."

This moment was not an honest one. It gave all appearances of being the last point at which the bloodshed to come could be avoided. That was a lie; the moment was a formality. There was nothing honest about it. What was about to happen had been decided long ago by two men who had not seen where their path would lead when they first stepped upon it.

"We are who we are," said the Knight. "I will not stand aside any more than you will walk away. Let's not make a show of this."

Philbreck nodded. "So be it." He drew a deep breath to bellow the order to advance.

The Knight Who Carried a Sword in His Heart raised his right hand to his chest, closed it around a hilt he could not see, but believed was there, and drew the sword from his heart. He felt every inch of it slide through his chest, a freezing, searing agony that stiffened every muscle in his body.

The Knight gritted his teeth against the pain. He believed in stories. He believed in magic. He believed in The Dreaming Tree and dragons and in himself. The blade came free, and the Knight held it out from his body. Silvered edges caught the morning sunlight and cut it in two. The sword was simple, as befitted a powerful weapon. It was marked only by a rough, broad crimson streak running the length of the blade, like the heartwood of a great cedar. A single drop of blood rolled off the tip and fell to the ground.

The Knight moved. He went from standing still to being in motion without appearing to move through any of the steps in between. Blood arced. Three men fell to the ground screaming, dying from wounds that appeared like magic. The Knight moved past them, secure in the knowledge they were no longer a threat.

The first rank charged, but they only had time for a single step before the Knight smashed into them. In seconds he was through that line as well, and every single soldier along the line was down. He moved through the ranks like blazing fire. His sword cut through armor and steel as easily as flesh, and it leant him both power and speed to fulfill its promise. No man could stand before him. Those farther back in the ranks had a few precious seconds to ready themselves. They struck out at the Knight, who wore no armor. The Knight accepted his wounds as the price of his decision and struck back with inhuman ferocity. He should have died quickly, but he fought with borrowed strength. The sword would keep him alive until his battle was finished. That was how the story went.

When the ranks broke, the Knight followed. He was violence given human form. No one who raised an arm against him could stand, and he left a river of blood in his wake that stopped only when he raised his sword against Abraham.

"I am not your enemy," Abraham said.

The Knight quivered with effort of holding back. He fell to his knees, bleeding from too many wounds to stay on his feet. The sword fed him strength, but every breath was agony, every movement torture.

Abraham slipped under the Knight's shoulder and bore his weight as he took the Knight back up to the mountain. He pressed a hand to the Knight's chest and felt the magic of the sword fading. At their feet, dying men moaned, begged for mercy, and clamored for help, all to no avail, but Abraham was intent upon assisting the Knight. The Knight had no mercy to give them.

A bloody hand grabbed the philosopher's robes. Abraham looked down to see Philbreck on his back, his other hand clutching at a terrible stomach wound. He gently lowered the Knight to the ground and knelt beside his lord.

"You promised...my father...you would watch out for me." Philbreck gasped out the words.

Abraham's heart hurt. He cupped Philbreck's face with his left hand so that the lord's eyes were focused on his face. "I tried, my lord." He had done his best, but in the end, Abraham could not save Philbreck from himself. The stomach wound was fatal, though death would be agonizing and slow to come. "All I can offer now is a vulgar mercy."

Philbreck's eyes widened. Abraham told himself it was a sign that he understood, though Abraham could not bring himself to believe Philbreck welcomed his end.

The knife in Abraham's right hand found Philbreck's heart. Abraham's vision blurred as he helped the Knight to his feet and led him to the mountain pass. The Knight tried to speak, to offer condolence or apology for Abraham's loss, but he was in too much pain to do so. He closed his eyes and trusted Abraham to guide him.

The next voice he heard was Byatt's.

"I never wanted this."

The Knight stirred at the sound of his friend's voice. He tried to speak, but he could only moan.

Byatt shifted, helpless. He desperately wanted to ease the Knight's pain, but there was nothing he could do for his friend in this form. He stilled himself, though his heart trembled as he watched the philosopher help the Knight lay down in the crook of Byatt's arm.

"You are safe, and you are home. You may rest now," Abraham said, the words the only benediction he could give.

The Knight opened his eyes and looked upon the sorrowful face of the dragon. The strength of the sword left him. The Knight knew his friend was safe and his battle was finished. He closed his eyes to rest at last.

"I did not ask for his," Byatt sobbed.

"You did not have to ask, Great One," Abraham said. "There is no greater love than this. He made his choice freely, and you bear no guilt. He wanted you to live in peace."

Byatt nuzzled the Knight. He lowered his head and rested it upon his forelegs, just as he had the night before. "A broken heart will have to be its own peace," said the dragon, and with these words, the last of the dragons passed from the world.

Grief overcame Abraham. He wept for Philbreck, for having failed Philbreck's father, for the men whose lives had been needlessly spent, and for the friendship that ended before him. Such moments were rare, and Abraham wept in awe of what he had witnessed and in regret for having seen it.

He knelt before Byatt and the Knight and pressed his palm to the stone floor. He spoke a word of magic, one he had learned long ago. Stone shifted and flowed like water, and the remains of the dragon and the knight sank into the floor. In their place rose a great statue, big enough to take up the entire chamber floor, of a dragon listening intently to a Knight reading from a book. There were no words inscribed upon the statue's base. The statue would speak for itself to any who cared enough to listen.

Abraham left the chamber, his heart heavy. When he left the tunnel, he turned back long enough to press his hand to the mountain. He spoke the word of magic again, this time with a different intonation, one that would add a layer of requirement to the stone that flowed like water.

Abraham sealed the mountain against the hope that someday a different dream would come to pass, one in which the world would again treasure everything that lay within, and left this dream behind.

See Joshua Hagy's story "The Knight Who Carried a Sword in His Heart" online at Metaphorosis.
If you liked it, leave a comment. Authors love that!
Remember to subscribe to our e-mail updates so you'll know when new stories are posted.

About the story

I've had a recurring dream/nightmare about a tree ever since I was a little kid. Sometimes it's a dream, but usually it's a nightmare. I've never been able to make sense of it, and in the last three years the tree has been showing up in my writing.

I was prepping for a production of *Macbeth* last year when the image of someone kneeling at the base of the tree like it was an altar came to me. I could see stars through the empty branches, and I knew the person left the tree with a sword hidden in his heart. knew the sword would give him purpose. I knew if he drew the sword from his heart, he would win the fight but die shortly after. There's something about a pyrrhic victory that's always appealed to me. I had to know what would make someone desperate enough to carry a sword in their heart and what would make them draw it, so I wrote to find out.

A question for the author

Q: If you could have any super power, what would it be?

A: I want the power to always say the right thing at the right time. Flight and super-strength are great, but I teach high school. I get a lot of questions from kids about life that I just can't answer. Among all the discussion raging about curriculum and distance learning and a million other things, you never really hear anyone talk about how to help the students with what they're going through. These are kids. Actual human beings. They have good days and bad days and terrible days, and they're still learning how to cope with it. As adults, we've forgotten what it means to be young and learning to face problems and pain. We tend to write their problems off as minor teenage problems that they'll get over, but they're dealing with so much more than we realize, and much of it on an adult level they shouldn't have to experience yet.

We lost a member of our senior class this year. I didn't have an answer to "Why did this happen?" or "How do I deal with this?" because there are no good answers. How am I supposed to know what to say to them when I still call my parents with the same questions? How am I supposed to help them when I don't understand, don't have the slightest idea of what to say to such pain? More than anything, I wish I had the power to always say the right words at the right time.

About the author

Joshua Hagy is a writer, high school and college English teacher, yearbook adviser, and theater director living and working in western Virginia. He's been lucky enough to have been married for nearly 14 years to his wife, Bethany, who has chosen to find his tendency to live inside his imagination amusing. When he isn't writing or working, Joshua spends his time searching for the perfect taco (he's already found the perfect pizza).

@The_Hagy23

We, You, and the Gallery

Alex Penland

We had thought ourselves safe, but then you found us in our little ship. There was a thrilling chase. In our desperation, we flew too fast and crashed, and you crashed too. Now we and you are both stranded on this empty, alien world. We do not know if you have survived. We know that only one of us remains, but we are still *we*, even when most of us are gone.

In your language, we believe, you sometimes say silence is *deafening*, but our experience is incongruous with that. The silence brings horrible clarity. In it, we are aware of the breathing which does not accompany our own, of the footsteps which do not fall around us, of the conversations which do not linger in our periphery. The silence is an illumination of all that we have lost.

We have buried the others by the cavern entrance. It is our hope that their decomposition will bring life to the dust of this barren world. Even near the subterranean spring there is nothing living here. No fish. No insects. No bacteria. Our scanners show a frustrating level of microbial safety.

It is there, by the spring, that we first speak to you. Your species needs water as desperately as ours does. Like us, you must have salvaged what you could from the wreckage and taken shelter in the caverns.

We do not know where you have hidden, but it's you who cries out—"Who's there?"—when we cause a thoughtless splash against the silence.

We are momentarily afraid, but we do not see you. The cavern is small; water rushes from one fissure into another. The only other point of entrance is the way from which we came. But for your voice, we seem to be alone.

"Where are you?" we ask. There are several sounds: one of your weapons firing, then the crumbling of rock, then a series of words my translator does not choose to divulge.

We think we understand. There is a phenomenon within caves: the chance alignment of reflective surfaces allows for sound to travel very far and very clearly. This must be the case now. You are not in the same cavern as we are; you might be miles away. You might be on the other side of the wall. There is no way of telling.

We test this by stepping briskly to the side. Your cursing fades to nothingness. When we return to the spot where we stood, your voice returns as well.

"It's a whispering gallery," we say into the anomaly. You stop shooting the walls.

"So you don't know where I am?"

"No."

"Great! So we can negotiate."

We're struck by your audacity. "Negotiate what?"

"Resources. Surrender. I don't know. How many of you are there?"

"We don't think we should say."

"Is that plural pronoun your hive-mind thing or does that mean there's more than one of you?"

We do not answer that.

"Well, assuming you're not alone, you got a resources issue. I got plenty of food, you know. Plus, I think I can get us outta here if you ask nice. You lot surrender and I'll get you a cushy cell 'til the war ends, I promise."

We do not answer that, either.

"Listen, it's better than dying out here, ain't it?"

"It is." We feel very alone. We wish desperately for our company, for the ability to talk this through together, but there is nothing to be done about that. "It is better than dying out here. Why would you bother to rescue us?"

This time you're the silent one.

"You need us alive," we say. "You need help too. We have no proof that you can help us. We have no proof that you will not slaughter us. So no, we do not surrender, and we will not tell you our location."

We step away from the gallery before we hear your reply. There is much to do; we have a ship to scavenge, inventory to document, plans to make. Possibly we have defenses to build. You are correct—we cannot survive here forever—but that does not mean we plan to die here, at either your hands or starvation's.

The room with the gallery is also the most defensible, and there is a nearby chamber that is cold enough for storage. We decide eventually to make this room our base, though during the process of moving supplies we make quite a lot of purposeful noise. You think we are numerous, after all.

Here it is dark and smells of sterile clay. Cool. Humid. The dead rock of the cavern is as much an absence as our silence. We ache for the fresh vegetation of home; the life in the air and the scent of the flowers.

But we cannot mourn. There is work to do.

Occasionally we see you. Once, while we deconstruct the refrigeration chamber in the wreckage of the ship, we spot your outline on a distant hill.

That night you say, "I saw one of you on the wreckage," and we reply that yes, you did, and hope you ask no further questions.

Once, when we venture out to scout a location for a distress signal, we find a machine of some sort, gathering sunlight. We steal it. That night you ask, "Did you steal one of my water purifiers?" and we reply that yes, we did.

Then we think it over. Perhaps you do not have the same access to water that we do. Perhaps you were unlucky. We feel a bit guilty. A few days later we return the machine without comment.

"What did you do to it?" you ask. We do not answer.

Once, we hear you crying.

We do not cry, though we have studied the phenomenon in school, so, although it takes a moment, we understand the sound. In your language, the convulsive gasp is a signal of despair. We do not think you meant to share it with us.

"Are you in distress?" we ask. You stop crying, or perhaps you move from the spot. You never respond to the question. We do not ask again.

One day we return to the wreckage site and you are standing there, arms crossed, waiting for us. You're male. Human, of course. Not as young as we thought you'd be, nor as well-armed. There's a pistol at your hip—it still smells of gunpowder from your duel with the cavern walls—but your ammunition belt is empty. Its grip is visible from your holster; the clip gauge on the side is blank. If you possess firepower, you possess only the shot in the chamber.

"Every time I see you out here, it's just you."

We are frozen to our location. We meet your eyes.

"You're alone, ain't you? You were lying. No one else survived the crash."

We hardly breathe.

"You had me pretty fooled. I was impressed." You hold out your hand. Are we supposed to shake it? We don't shake it. "I'm Edwin. You got a name?"

"Do your fingertips have names?" we ask. "Do your hands?"

"I call 'em Left and Right, generally. So... no? No name?"

"No name."

"Why do you say *we*?"

"Your hand is still your hand, even if we were to cut it from your body."

You nod. You glance behind yourself, back towards the way we suspect you came. "I'm gonna call you Honeybee."

"What?"

"You're a hive alien. You look like bees. You ever see a bee?"

"We are not a bee."

"I'm not saying you are. It's just a name. I gotta call you something. Like it or not, we're both stuck here."

We aren't opposed to names, really. Our opposition is to *you*, not your customs. Honeybee. Hm. "Are we? Didn't you say you had a way out?"

"Thought I did. Turned out I didn't."

"Hm." We lean next to you against the ship. "Neither do we. What was your plan?"

"Originally I was gonna steal components off your ship, but then you gave me back the water purifier." You sigh. "You ain't gonna surrender. I sure as hell ain't gonna surrender. So what now?"

"You have food, but no water?" we ask.

"Yup."

"We have water, but our food is running out. In our language, we say that it is better to die as a community than to live a longer life alone." By the odd look you give us, we suspect you understand the situational irony. "By this we mean that we risk a shortened life by offering to trust you, but if we rely only on ourself, our expiration date is certain."

You work through that for a moment. "You suggesting we share?"

"Yes. Return here tomorrow. We will bring you water."

"And then what?"

We shrug. "Show us your resources. Show us your ship. We're making the choice to trust you. Trust us in return, and we'll plan our escape together."

You look surprised, and a little wary, but you offer us your hand again. This time we do shake it.

"All right," you say. "Good to meet you, Honeybee."

"Good to meet you, Edwin."

This is what you possess: a truly massive cache of rations (roughly half of which are toxic to our biology, which makes division simple), three water purifiers, and half a ship. You do not have the same electrical and engineering knowledge that we do, and we suspect that you would simply have stranded us both if you tried to dismantle our ship to fix your own. You need us more than we need you, we think.

"There are elements we can work with," we say, perusing your technology, "but it's going to take a while. We'll be in a race for time with food."

"And by we, you mean you."

"Unless you can learn engineering on the fly." You laugh. "I have another job for you. As your rations consist of processed bars—"

"Don't give me that judgy tone."

"—*they cannot be farmed*, whereas our rations contain seeds, and likewise will rot sooner. We suggest that you attempt to farm some of our rations while we repair your ship, and that we subsist on your rations in the meantime. Our food grows quickly. It's meant for this exact scenario."

"We're repairing my ship?"

"Ours has been stripped more thoroughly. We believe yours is a more functional base." We replace the panel we were inspecting and stand to meet your eyes. "We are risking quite a lot to help you, Edwin. We understand that humanity is... individualistic..."

"We comprise individuals, yeah."

"And it is out of respect for you, as an individual, that we are trusting you will not make the same collective choice as your species."

You frown.

"Namely, that you will not choose war. That you will treat us, together, as a collective for the time being. Our good will be your good. Your good will be our good. We will become a community, not a pair of individuals at war."

"You know we have communities back home, yeah? I ain't unfamiliar with the concept."

"As far as we can tell, your hives are constantly in swarm."

You pause, then laugh. "Fair point. I won't screw you over. I'll even let you go free. When we get this fixed we head to the nearest neutral world and part ways. On my word, all right?"

We wince. We do not like the idea of landing on a neutral world, especially not alone. They are dangerous and unpredictable in their diversity. "Forgive us, please, but your word means very little. We will trust in cause and effect."

"What?"

"We will see what happens and how you react. We will see how you respond to the situation we have found ourselves in. As time passes, we will learn the mark you choose to leave upon the world. This is the information we need in order to determine the value of your word."

"Again—what?"

"Trust takes time, Edwin. We simply do not know you yet. This is a dangerous decision, but one we are making consciously. Do not attempt to put us at ease with promises we have no way of validating."

You shrug, scratch your neck, survey the desolation of our surroundings. "All right. Guess I can't blame you for that."

Time occurs. Days pass, then weeks. You are proving to be an adept farmer, particularly when faced with our fast-growing crops. Our rations are quick and hardy—they can be grown nearly anywhere, and the sweet resin which compacts them doubles as nutrition for whatever soil one can find. Like us, they are less tolerant to heat, but there is a cavern protected from the midday sun that still has some ambient light. We cart in sand from the surface.

The first harvest, one month in, allows us to set aside the remaining ration bars for an emergency supply. The second harvest, two weeks later, allows us to dry fruit for storage. By the third, we have more food than we can eat.

We begin to enjoy our meals together. At first, this is only in shared spaces—the ship, or sometimes outdoors when the weather is bearable.

Over time, however, you introduce us slowly to your space. You reveal that you have inhabited a cave on the far side of the hill. We suspect that you did not survey your surroundings when you crashed, but rather picked a direction to walk in and colonized the first cave you found. It is not nearby. It is not easily defensible. It is well-hidden, to your credit, but only because no tactical mind would choose to hide there.

We do not tell you this. Instead we express our honor when we are allowed to observe the mementos tucked beside your bed, the books piled in corners, the stringed instrument you rescued from the wreckage. It is not clean. The odor of your dirty laundry makes our antennae curl.

Yet you have built furniture: a desk, a lifted bed, storage in unexpected places. It is more confined than our cavern, but you have built an ingenious home in very little space. We are fascinated.

We are also often frustrated, though somehow not by you. When working, we are challenged by the incompatibilities between our two technologies. While hardware is obedient under the pressure of brute force, software is less pliable. Our universal translator is decidedly unhelpful when it comes to programming languages —as are you.

Today, as I swear at the translator, you don't offer to assist; you watch and laugh until we enter a command. The engine roars threateningly, which stops your teasing.

"Are you wasting fuel at me, Honeybee?"

"You can laugh, or you can help."

You're about to respond, but there's a jolt against the side of the ship that has nothing to do with software. You're at the window before we can turn around. The sand on the ground is blowing. The wind's picked up.

In the distance the air has begun to shimmer: heat. Intense, visible heat. You stick your head out the door to observe and burn your hand on the outer wall of the ship. A smell of singed flesh flashes through the bridge. Another untranslatable word—you duck back in.

"Hey, Honeybee, got a fun fact for ya. My life support's down."

"We are aware." We're trying to assess if we've fixed that yet. The translator is currently displaying the code in front of us as a list of various species of snake.

"Did you fix it?"

"We... aren't sure."

"You think we can make it to a cave from here?"

"We aren't sure, Edwin."

"Well, when you gonna know?" We open our mouth to respond. You don't let us say it again. "Right. Come on. We're making a break for the caves. Now."

We look up from the computer. You're holding out a hand, halfway out the door already.

"Come on. I ain't leaving without you."

"Is it close enough? Will we make it?"

"I ain't sure."

The storm is at our back. We try to fly you, to move more quickly, but our wings blister when they spread. When the pair of us dive into the caverns we are afraid, for a moment, that they will not provide adequate protection, but you drag us further below the surface and pat out the charring on our clothes. We press ourself against the cool ground and shiver. In your language you would say we are 'gasping for air'. We are not sure that this translates directly to our circulatory system, but the intent behind the words is accurate.

We suspect you are more resilient to heat than we are. You are leaning against the wall, sweating, breathing, staring at the inferno that rages outside.

It becomes slowly apparent to us that you have led us to our cave, not yours. It was the closer of the two dwellings; it was also a tactical mistake, to bring yourself to our territory. The action suggests trust. Behind the dull exhaustion of the heat, we are conflicted.

"Think we've figured out why nothing lives here, Honeybee."

We nod, still fragile from the storm.

"You all right?"

We haul ourself to a sitting position. It seems dangerous to tell you that we are vulnerable to temperatures—we do not know what information will be reported to your superiors. To risk our life is one thing; to put all of us at risk is another. And yet you chose our survival over your advantage.

"Bee, look at me."

But we are weak. We feel a strange, trembling headache, and our body is enervated. When we look at you we do not register your expression. When we fall, we do not register your catching us. The world fades.

There is a sound of rushing water.

We have cooled significantly. Before we open our eyes we can feel our hands and feet are submerged, though our body lies on cold stone. We realize what has happened—you have saved our life, at least temporarily. We had overheated; now we have cooled.

We have perhaps cooled too much. We sit up, slowly, battling the lethargy in our joints. Heat makes us weak; cold makes us heavy. Our blood feels like syrup in our veins.

You made a fire some time ago; it has now dwindled into embers. The smoke still trails along the ceiling, leaving chemical traces in the air. You yourself are currently sleeping on my bed, having covered yourself in empty ration canvas to keep in the heat from your warm-blooded body.

Unlike you, Edwin, we do not generate heat well. Our bodies are more vulnerable to environmental conditions. We need warmth. Unthinking, we crawl across the cavern—we do not have the strength to walk—and bury ourself in the bed beside you. When we rest our forehead on your back, you are like a lantern on a cold and unforgiving night. Then you turn in your sleep and wrap your arms around us, and the lantern blossoms into the sun.

When we wake again, you have rekindled the fire (we wonder how long you searched for our fire kit, how long it took you to recognize it for what it was) and you are cooking fruit on a griddle. The cavern smells like toasted sugar, tart and syrupy. We lay here quietly, watching the scene.

You do not seem alien to us in this moment. You are humming an alien tune, tapping the matte luster of your fingers on alien knees, but there is a familiarity in the domesticity of cooking. We are reminded of morning meals in the cafeteria hall, of baking and frying-up in our rotations of a dozen-or-so individuals. We are reminded of the easy chemistry between ourselves, of the casual warmth and connection of the collective.

We are momentarily and intensely homesick.

"Hey, Honeybee. You alive over there?"

You've noticed. We nod, reluctant to leave the lingering comfort of the bed. We think our thermoregulation has balanced itself, but this is comfortable, and we are very tired.

"You had me worried."

"We were very lucky you knew how to do first aid." We were, in fact, surprised. You knew to put our hands and feet in the water; if you had placed our body, as human anatomy directs, we would have drowned. "How did you know how to save us?"

"I'm military, Bee. We do get training."

"In human medicine, certainly. We are not human."

"We get alien basics, too. You know we've got some of you lot on our side, right? Defectors. Not everyone loves the hive."

The horror is plain on our face, or perhaps the despair.

"Don't look at me like that! We treat 'em right. If someone wants to be an individual, let 'em."

"We simply cannot imagine the desire." There is a spot near the fire where you have folded a mat for us to sit on, and we sit there now. "Having lost our connection to the hive, we cannot fathom the decision one must make to leave willingly. One would lose everything."

"How can you know that? You don't know their whole situation. You don't know what they've been through."

"We have lost everything, Edwin."

"Ah. Right. Sorry." You pause. "You ain't alone. Uh. Lost my own family to a hive attack."

"Did you?"

"It was years ago, so... You know. War's not... great."

You clear your throat uncomfortably. I change the subject.

"Arrowfruit tastes quite good when paired with redspice."

"What?"

"What you're cooking. Arrowfruit. We believe there is some redspice left in the stores—"

"That's what, the red powder?"

"Purple, actually. The name misleads."

We retrieve the bag, and the pair of us begin to cook together.

That first day of the storm, once we have eaten and checked the status of the weather, we take stock together of what we possess.

There are enough rations to get us through quite some time. Together we venture closer to the entrance to check on the crops; their cavern is much warmer than it has been previously, but not so warm as to cause them harm. We have water from the spring. We are not sure how long the storm will last, but our basic needs for survival are met.

Next, comfort. We are in our own territory, but you only have what you've carried in your bag. It is admittedly heavy, but it is always on your person and you tend to carry your tools with you: a small multi-device you call a *pocket knife*, extra rations in case you were to become stuck somewhere for a while, and most importantly a spare set of clothes.

You chuckle at our visible relief. "What, you don't like how I smell?"

"We were taking into consideration that your living quarters smell quite strongly of human body odor."

"It's not like I got a shower in there!"

"And do you have a similar excuse for your ship?" Our antennae curl. "We understand that you have a dulled sense of smell. We can forgive that. We're simply appreciative that we won't have to live with it."

"It ain't that bad."

"Not to you."

You also have a deck of playing cards.

You attempt to teach us the game of *poker*, which does not go particularly well. When you run out of the pebbles you've insisted on gambling with, we offer you some of ours. We receive in turn a lecture on how we are missing the point, to which we reply we have clearly won the game and ask how much of the point we can possibly be missing, and it is at this point that you decide to find a project rather than a game to play.

The phrase in your language is *sore loser.*

You decide to 'spruce up' our living space, starting with the bed. We have been sleeping on a pile of mats, which is quite comfortable, but—

"Listen, if I'm staying here, I ain't sleepin' on the floor. I'm making you a bedframe."

Implicit in this decision is the implication that we will be sharing a bed again. We are not sure how we feel about that assumption. Certainly it was comfortable. Certainly you did not kill us in our sleep, or in our illness, and you had the chance to do so. Your gun lies near the cavern entrance, a single shot still loaded in the chamber.

And yet we wonder whether bed-sharing contains the same implications for you as it does for us—do your people cluster the way we do? Do your people bond together, form lifelong connections? Or are your romances as individualistic and flighty as the rest of your culture? Are you, Edwin, like the rest of your people? Is there even something that can be defined as 'the rest of your people'? Are we simply overthinking things?

"We are not ectothermic," we explain eventually, watching you consolidate supplies and tear apart crates. "We are capable of sleeping alone if you wish to bed down elsewhere."

You shrug. "It's no bother."

"Are you sure?"

" 'Course."

And the matter is settled.

On the second day of the storm, we teach you our games. We spend some time carving a set of horribly unbalanced dice from spare parts of the bed project, then show you how to use them. You enjoy dare-dice best, where we take turns suggesting a task and then roll to see who must perform it.

The game is generally used to allocate horrible chores back home, but we are stuck in a small and mostly-featureless room, and so dares quickly become questions.

We begin to learn about each other.

The weirdest thing you've ever eaten: sawdust, when you were in particularly dire straits on a survivalist training exercise.

The most memorable dream we've ever had: it occurred the night before we began our military training, when we dreamed we were a comet sailing peacefully through the universe. When we awoke, we had a distinct memory of a bright light on a horizon that could not have existed, and a longing for understanding that would never come.

Your childhood dream: you wanted to be a space pirate.

Our favorite color: starlight. Pale and shining flecks against the black.

Your most embarrassing moment: you were a child. Your older sister once called you *Ed-lose*, and it upset you so much you cried and threw up your dinner. You no longer speak with your sister, but you insist that is not the primary reason.

You ask us what we would have done if we had not joined the military, which is confusing. Then it occurs to us that you believe that soldiers are different from ordinary citizens. We find this disheartening. If your citizens are not the same as those who fight, and your people are individuals, how can you truly understand the cost of war?

"Maybe," you say. "But I think if I weren't in the military I'd be something real dull, which, well, I guess some people might want to do that with their lives."

"Why was this the life you chose?" we ask, abandoning the dice. "Why would anyone choose war?"

You're quiet about that for a while, leaning back against the cavern wall. For a little bit the only sounds are those of the subterranean spring and the distant chaos of the storm. We allow you your time to think, observing you instead. We have become familiar with your face, with the softness of your body. Your appearance has begun to bring us comfort, and that is a frightening thing.

We wonder if perhaps others have not abandoned their communities, but simply chosen new ones.

"I didn't really choose it," you admit. "The military's a shit job, so people in shit situations are the ones who sign up. You get a good deal—good money, good education, good place to lay your head. I didn't have any of that when I signed up. I do now. Not sure it's worth the golden chains, though."

"Do you regret it?"

"I did." There's an invisible edge to your answer, somehow. Something clinging behind the words, something which makes our back flutter, which brings a shiver to our fingertips.

We lean forward. "Do you regret it now?"

"You know, Honeybee? I ain't sure."

The storm rages on. Days blend together. Time passes.

At night we sleep encircled in the safety of your arms. At first we refuse to talk about this during the day, but then you put your arm around us in a moment of sympathy, and we lean our head on your shoulder, and the physical barrier is broken. What was relegated to sleep becomes common. We sit together. We eat together.

We are no longer alone.

We are awoken by a faint and repeated alarm. We roll over, bleary, to ask you if you recognize the signal. You are not there.

We sit up. We are surprised and a little confused.

The situation makes more sense once we realize the noise is coming from the whispering gallery, and once we realize we can no longer hear the storm outside. It is one of your devices, then, and the world outside is safe for passage. You have returned to your cavern to retrieve it. There is nothing suspicious or unexpected about that.

And so we take the time to think.

This bond we've formed with you, whatever it may be—we know it's doomed. We asked you to consider our pair as a community, and while we meant that, it was not intended to be mutual. For us to consider you the same is—

It's dangerous. There is no other word for it. We do not part from our community, and upon leaving we must part from you. You have shown no inclination towards joining our hive; we cannot bear to join your swarm. There is no future in which we stay together.

And yet we lie back down and soak in the warmth you left behind. The echo of footsteps that are not there have grown softer in your presence. The silence is no longer intrusive. We cannot deny the change.

Last night you placed your hand on our chest and asked us where our heartbeat was. When we didn't know what you were talking about, you placed *our* hand on *your* chest in demonstration. We laughed; we told you how we have a dozen small hearts down our abdomen, explained our circular breathing. Wasn't that covered in your training? But you say you only learned the protocol, not the biology.

You placed your hand upon each heart of ours and felt its rhythm. You called us fascinating. You called us beautiful.

Love is a state of neutrality in the hive. We are always perfectly in sync; it is the glue which seals our metaphorical cells, a propolis of the soul. We join sometimes— mostly in twos, sometimes more—but to do so is to entwine two threads within the greater aegis of the soul. Beautiful, yes, divine, but not a source of conflict.

We are accustomed to love, accustomed to connection, and yet somehow entirely unsettled by the feelings you inspire in us. When we speak, we argue as much as we admire; when we fight we are drawn together more than we are repulsed. Everything you are opposes the virtues we were raised on, and yet this only seems to draw us closer.

We asked you, yesterday, what your greatest childhood fear had been. You said: us. The hive. We were the ones who killed your family. (Just as you killed ours. We have forgiven, not forgotten.) But you are no longer afraid.

We are. We are terrified.

We do not want to leave this community.

We do not want to leave you.

We have drifted back to sleep again. This time we are awoken by your distant voice, and this time you are not alone.

"Sorry," you say through the gallery echo, "I didn't quite catch that. Can you state your name and ID again?"

"This is Jeffrey Reynolds, ID 809192-9."

"Hey there, Jeff. Good to hear your voice, it's been a hot minute out here."

"We got your distress call, Ed. What happened? We thought you were a goner."

"Oh, nothing too special. Took a dumb chance chasing some..." You hesitate. We know your language. We can hear the habitual use of *bugs* on your lips, and we hear you repress it. "Took a dumb chance on a chase and we both crashed."

"Any bugs get out?"

You hesitate. We understand. You can tell them we all died, and we would be safe. We could leave on the repaired ship and this man could send rescue for you. But we suspect you want us to defect, that you do not want to part ways either. You will want to know what our options are.

"Yeah," you say. "The crash didn't get 'em all. But don't you worry, we're all gettin' on good. Say Jeff, you know how the asylum process works? Think I'd be able to offer my friends here a deal?"

"Sure, probably. Citizenship in exchange for time served against the Hive. Standard." We can hear the disgust in your friend's tone. "Sure happy to turn a blind eye if you squash the bastards before we get there, though. All those legs. Ugh. Freaks me out."

"Well, guess we have differing opinions on that." Your voice has gone cold, polite. "What would asylum look like?"

"Can't say as for sure, man. Tell you what, send me your coordinates and I'll make sure there's a specialist on board, huh? Give 'em a good deal?"

"Certainly." You pause again. "Uh, you know what, Jeff, I gotta go find those coordinates exactly, they're still on my ship. I'll get 'em back to you soon, yeah?"

"You don't have them with you?" Jeff's surprise is warranted. You absolutely have them with you. You are likely looking at them, taped to your cavern wall, right in your eyeline. "Right. Yeah. Sure. You can leave the signal on too and we can track—"

There is an audible click.

"Turned it off," you say. "I can't bear that guy. You catch all that, Honeybee?"

"We did."

We are aware you could have deceived us. We can think of a dozen ways that conversation could be faked, and a dozen reasons why. We think of the round you left in the chamber. The gun is with us now; you did not bring it with you when you went to answer the call.

You are an individual; this does not mean your choices are selfish. You have chosen only once to cause us harm, before you knew us. You have kept us safe a dozen times since. Time has passed, and we have seen the mark you choose to leave upon the world.

We pick up your weapon and turn it over in our hands. It has never been used for violence against us. You are the only thing which has been profaned in such a way.

We say: "We do not wish to join your military."

"I know, Honeybee. Just wanted to know what our options were." You exhale. "I don't want to fight my people either."

"And similarly, you would be required to if you joined us."

"Of course." You're quiet again for a moment, thinking. "Before we make a decision, we should check the ship. See what damage the heat did. See if we have any other choice, you know?"

We stand together in front of the ship.

It's fine.

It's absolutely fine.

Our ship—that is, the hive ship—has melted irreparably. It is a twisted and deformed hunk of metal and wax, a final monument to those of us who died in its crash. Eventually, future storms will smear it across the face of the planet, and it will be gone forever.

But your ship? Your ship is pristine.

"How?" you ask. We are already climbing in through the hatch, assessing. "What did you do to it? It looks better than when we left it—"

"It's not better," we say, "but it appears we did, in fact, fix the life support before the storm hit. The interior was able to protect itself. We had also connected our shields with yours, and that seems to have been a miraculous success, though it's built to withstand far more intense heat on atmospheric interaction."

"Well, that's good."

"In fact," — we peer out from the hatch again — "we think our work is done."

"Done?"

"Done. Complete. The ship is low on fuel, there are a dozen bugs in the software, but we believe a trip to the nearest neutral planet would be viable."

You're staring at us.

"Edwin?"

"So that's it?" you ask.

"What?"

"You're leaving?" There's a panicked shiver to your voice.

"We didn't say that. We said the ship is viable. We..." We leave the words unspoken. We aren't sure what we were going to say, anyway. "There are decisions to be made, that's all."

"Yeah." You glance up at the sky. It's brightening; a brilliant blue after the firestorm.

We hesitate before speaking again. "We do not wish to part ways, Edwin."

You exhale. "No. We don't."

"And yet we don't wish to fight our own people."

"No, we don't."

We sit on the ground, leaning against the ship, looking out at the wasteland that has become something like a home. Your breathing is slow and even; mine is a low hum against a background breeze. Our hands brush accidentally. We exchange a glance of quiet desolation.

"We wonder when you started referring to us as a plural."

You roll your eyes.

"You think of us as a pair."

"Yeah, I do. Don't you?"

We close our eyes, thinking of our past pairings, thinking of the hive. We nod. We think perhaps that the two of us are more a pair than any other person we have loved. It is a dangerous thought.

"Listen," you say, "I don't know how they do this in the hive. I don't know if you just... love free, or only love your queen, or how it works, but humans, when we choose someone else— Well, we got a thousand different ways to fall in love, but where I'm from it's usually just... We pick the other individual we love best, and we make our choices from there."

To be loved best seems impossible. One is not meant to be loved best. One is meant to sacrificed for all, not sacrificed for. The image of the pair of us in our patchwork ship, running from our people, hiding out in the wild diversity of the neutral planets—it surfaces in our mind and we cannot dislodge it.

We imagine what it would be like, to travel the stars and trust only in each other. We imagine love rife with conflict and passion. We imagine life, free and forlorn but never lonely.

Never lonely. Not with you.

We cannot bear to open our eyes, to see the look upon your face. Perhaps it is not as desperately fond as your voice; perhaps there is not the same helpless affection. Perhaps you are lying. We could not survive it, if you were lying. We have changed too much by loving you to be the person that we were.

"And sometimes that individual changes, Honeybee, I won't lie about that. But I don't know you as the collective, right? I know you as Honeybee. And Bee, I love you best. Easily. I love you best."

We open our eyes. You are not lying. We reach out to clean the tears from your cheek. Our hand is unsteady.

"I can't fight 'em," you say, "but I can't go back, either. If we don't want to split up, if you'll have me…"

"This is our collective," we whisper. "Us."

We have buried the others by the cavern entrance. Our hive seems very far away, and you are close, and you are also fascinating, and you are also beautiful.

"Us," you say.

It is dangerous, and perhaps it is ill-advised, but you never send the coordinates to your superior. Instead, we make our preparations. You harvest the last of our crops: a bit dry, a bit small, but survivors of the storm. We gather a list of neutral planets—an eclectic bouquet of utopias and university worlds, of war-torn dust-traps and regressed historical inaccuracies, of oceans and jungles and constructed habitats. They are unpredictable, but so are you. Perhaps unpredictable does not always indicate danger.

Our first task is to repair our ship beyond a state of limping; after that, we will take to the void. We will have our choice of worlds; we will have our choice of stars.

When the time comes, we chart our course and leave.

We leave together.

On an abandoned, uninhabitable planet, there are several shallow graves. There is, for now, the wreckage of a single spaceship, slowly deteriorating in a harsh and unforgiving climate. In the myriad caves below the surface, there are wild fruits which drink from natural aquifers. They can be found safe in the shade, growing wherever the last traces of light will touch them.

There is a cavern. In it are the scattered traces of habitation; a charred fire pit, broken boards, a bed which was gratefully abandoned. On the wall, we have carved one message in two languages. The engravings are side by side.

We have written:

"In this place, violence was supplanted by love. May the universe share our same conclusion."

Below our message, you have fired a single shot into the wall.

See Alex Penland's story "We, You, and the Gallery" online at Metaphorosis.
If you liked it, leave a comment. Authors love that!
Remember to subscribe to our e-mail updates so you'll know when new stories are posted.

About the story

In 2022, sometime in January, my grandfather died and my father was diagnosed with an aggressive form of cancer. But "We, You, and the Gallery" isn't a cancer story.

In 2019, just before the pandemic hit, I left the US and moved to Scotland to pursue my degrees in writing. The world closed down six months later. I didn't want to risk my family by returning home, so I chose to remain in the UK. When I made the choice, I fell against the wall and cried until I ran out of tears. But "We, You, and the Gallery" isn't a pandemic story.

In 2022 again, sometime in March, war broke out in Europe. I spent that uneasy week staring out my window, writing pieces of an opera about Odysseus. My eyes rested on a carving in Grassmarket where a bomb fell in World War II. "We, You, and the Gallery" is a war story. That one I'll give you.

When my father started chemotherapy, something in me broke. My family is close—they're my we, whether or not I'm with them—and the thought of losing him at a distance was too much to bear. War and plague weren't enough to break my practicality, but when faced with loss, the risk was far too great. I spent the next few months in America, staying with my dad on his good weeks and with my mom when the chemo hit hardest. He was in good hands. I was there to cheer him up, not to get in his way.

This is the environment in which "We, You, and the Gallery" was written. I was surrounded by hurt, and death, and fear. (So were we all.) My hometown, where my mother lives, was on the verge of spring— dogwoods and cherry trees all just beginning to blossom. There was plastic drifting down the gutter streams. There had been so little snow last year. The world was wet and covered in a vivid green, and everyone, everywhere, was dying.

I'm not sure where I got the idea. I don't know where Edwin and Honeybee came from.

All I know is that one day I came downstairs in the morning—I was at my mother's house—and they were in my mind. Suddenly I knew this story about love that sparks between differences—because of differences. Reality was raw and bleeding. Love was fending it off with a busted lip and a black eye, but still fighting. This was true of real life and fiction alike. I needed to remember that. I needed to write about it.

The first draft took a single day. The second draft was done at my father's house and took a further two days; it expanded the story by several thousand words. I've put it through further edits since then (to say nothing of the incredible feedback provided by *Metaphorosis* itself), but I have never produced a workable draft so quickly.

I don't know where "We, You, and the Gallery" came from, but I needed it. I'm so glad I've had the chance to share the tale with you.

A question for the author

Q: What's your favorite type of pie?

A: For a couple years now, I've been learning my mother's pie crust recipe from across the pond. I'm originally from Washington, DC, so of course as soon as I moved to Scotland I realized how much I missed it; she essentially just uses pastry dough. It's incredible. Especially when she bakes it in one of those tins with the holes all over it. I don't mind if it's pumpkin or apple or chicken pot pie, but that crust is essential.

About the author

Alex Penland is a former museum kid. They spent their childhood running rampant through the Smithsonian museums, which kicked off an early career as a child adventurer. Alex has worked in the field with NASA scientists, linguists, and acclaimed photographers. Now a Pushcart-nominated author, Alex currently lives in Scotland while studying for a PhD in Creative Writing at the University of Edinburgh. They still run rampant, but they've breached the Smithsonian's containment.

www.AlexPenland.com, @AlexPenname

The Zoo Diaries

Frances Pauli

Part One

The Rainriver Zoological Gardens are fully licensed and operate in accordance with the Animal Welfare Act and the Endangered Species Act, which set minimum standards for the care and keeping of animal exhibits. In compliance with the law, each enclosure is designed to meet the minimum requirements for the animal within it. Each diet is planned to satisfy the minimum goals for health and vitality, and each animal is cared for, handled, and transported in a fashion that meets the minimum conditions for humane treatment.

The zoo was once a popular tourist destination. It was once awarded a prestigious accolade for its public outreach and overall design.

Recently, it has fallen upon financial difficulties that make providing *minimum* care a constant juggling act between obeying the laws and keeping the doors open.

Ape House

Gonzo the macaque smells the coffee long before he can see it. The-one-who-sweeps-the-walks passes in front of his territory. She clutches the broom in her odd, hairless fist. The other hand holds the vessel, and the vessel emits the thick, overpowering scent of *bean.*

Gonzo's paws tremble. His nostrils gape, reaching for the scent as if the fumes alone could sustain him. He salivates. His lips stretch back, revealing stained teeth, four-centimeter fangs, and a pink tongue. His head throbs. It has been four months since he chewed the bean. Four months of hell.

Outside his range, a wretched crow perches like death atop the 'Jungle' sign. She caws, a nail straight through Gonzo's caffeine-deprived skull. She caws, and the macaque cringes.

Tortoise Enclosure

Oliver drags a stumpy leg through the sand. He pulls, one clawed foot at a time, flicking sharply at the last second so that a shower of grit washes away behind his great domed shell.

He digs. He rocks forward and back. He is 110 years old.

Today he's circled his enclosure three times already, but Miranda has not returned. She does not hide behind the prickly cactus. She does not wade in the shallow pool. She is not stalking through the reeds near the square door that leads nowhere.

She is missing.
Oliver drags at the sand. He digs.
The love of his long life has vanished.

MEMO: ALL ZOO STAFF

THIS IS A REMINDER TO ALL PARK EMPLOYEES NOT TO FEED THE NATIVE FAUNA.

AS YOU ARE AWARE FROM THE PIGEON INCIDENT, THESE SITUATIONS CAN QUICKLY GET OUT OF HAND, CAUSING DAMAGE TO ZOO PROPERTY AND ENDANGERING THE WELFARE OF OUR GUESTS.

WE HAVE RECEIVED COMPLAINTS ABOUT THE AGGRESSIVE NATURE OF THE PARK BIRDS ALREADY, AND IT IS VITAL THAT WE ARE PROACTIVE AND DIFFUSE THE SITUATION BEFORE IT ESCALATES.

ANY EMPLOYEE CAUGHT FEEDING THE CROWS WILL BE SUBJECT TO DISCIPLINARY ACTION.

Elephant Paddock

Shanti calculates the width of her enclosure in steps. She measures the length and deduces the height of her shelter by triangulation. Her trunk lays out bits of straw to represent each distance. She bundles them, divides, and reorganizes her square footage.

There are thirty-seven peanuts in a pile beside the straw. She has gathered and counted them. The crowd threw 168 peanuts. She has eaten 131.

Curling her trunk into an ess, she flaps her flat ears and blows out a reverberating sigh. If she saved 100 peanuts, in ten days she would have a thousand.

She stuffs three into her mouth, subtracts them from her total. Calculates.

There are seven zebras in the enclosure beside hers. If each zebra has twenty stripes…

The Crow

The macaque throws a stone at her. Debra shrieks and takes to wing. Perhaps it was only a carrot nub, a lump of rind or vegetable scrap left over from his morning meal. She flies anyway, lets the pigeons have it.

Down from the apes, the trundling Sulcata tortoise, Oliver, is attempting to escape again. Debra teases him until he begins to cry. Then she tires and circles.

She flies over the Savannah, past the elephant, the arctic wedge, and the cat house. Somewhere behind this she can hear the hyena sobbing. Debra ignores that sport, landing instead upon the peak of the great aviary.

Her brethren amass there. The irony of it amuses them. A full murder of free crows huddling atop the massive avian jail. Debra joins them long enough to add her stories to the morning's gossip. Then she hops to the roof's edge and waits at the highest point above the building's double-glass doors.

Soon, the park will open. Soon the hordes will enter.

They will push their strollers through the stiles, purchase warm bags of popcorn, piping hot lattes. They will steer their infants down the paths to the double-glass and find for the first time the sign which reads: 'No Strollers'.

The children will wail. The door will open and close, releasing for a brief moment the many calls of the birds trapped inside. Then, a line of abandoned strollers will wait below, overflowing with treats and ripe for plunder.

Debra loves popcorn.

And though the crowds have been much thinner of late, though the walks are less choked and the spoils less plentiful, she will drink from someone's latte today. She will think of the macaque dreaming of his beans and laugh.

A solitary pigeon, brave or suicidal, streaks past the aviary. The murder shifts, caws, and threatens.

"Watch out," the fat gray body calls back. "Watch. Watch."

The crows hop and posture but do not fly. Do not chase. The gates are open now, and they are not fools.

Hyena Pen

Today her cubs are six months old. Alice has not seen them in two weeks. She opens her square jaws and lets loose a sobbing cackle. Her teats have long since dried, but she is certain there were two healthy, viable cubs. She remembers them, and her spotted fur bristles.

Two cubs with strong, sloping backs once bounced and gamboled in the cramped, square enclosure. Two sang with her, obeyed her as their mother and matriarch.

Alice climbs to the top of her stair-step rock and lowers her head to the cold, too-smooth stone.

She can smell them beneath the harsh, biting disinfectant. She can smell her family, and she knows, for a moment, that they were real.

Grizzly Grotto

Hector works at a bur that is stuck deep in his shaggy pelt. The sticker has lodged just behind his left elbow, and he is forced to stretch to reach it, to contort his massive body so that his long, sickle-shaped claws can scratch and pry at the thing.

He growls and ripples his black lips. His ears lie flat against his huge skull, and the nub of his tail tucks tight against his round bottom.

He sits up, glares at the trench that surrounds his home. A fat log lies on this side, a broken stump stands beside him. Hector considers trundling over, using the bare wood to scratch away his irritation.

He considers it, but *she* will arrive soon, and tree scratching is far too undignified for a bear of his stature.

Already he hears the noises. Pattering feet and barking voices. Hector listens, lifting his face high and scenting for her.

She is always early, and he has learned to wake long before his body's rhythm would prefer. He groans at the ache in his right hip, but he leaves off scratching and finds a more dignified pose.

She appears at the railing high above the trench. By then, he is rampant, stretching tall on his hind legs and only gripping the leaning stump with one paw for balance. He is mighty. He is bear.

She claps her hands once for him, takes out her pencil and her book, and begins to draw.

RAINRIVER ZOOLOGICAL GARDENS

NUTRITIONAL RECORD: AFRICAN LION
   (2X DAILY PLUS ENRICHMENT)
   SUN/AM BEEF HAUNCH   PM
COMMERCIAL MINCE
   MON/AM   BLOOD   BLOCK(FROZ)
      PM MINCE
   TUE/AM   BEEF   CUBES/FEMUR
      PM MINCE
   WED/AM MINCE / ZEBRA DUNG
      PM MINCE
   THU/AM ZEBRA HAUNCH
      PM MINCE
   FRI/AM MINCE
      PM MINCE

SAT/AM MINCE / DUNG   PM
MINCE

HEALTH CONCERNS: NONE

THE BOARD

The board of directors discusses migrating the largest predators to a diet of commercial mince, which is far more cost effective, and according to the sales brochure provides a well-balanced and nutritional substitute. Someone points out the deficiency in mental enrichment and stimulus, but a solution is negotiated. The mince will be supplemented with blocks of frozen cow's blood.

When these blood blocks are introduced into the enclosures, they are well received. Everyone's worries are assuaged, and the money saved goes to a remodel of the front gates designed to increase the facility's curb appeal.

Lion Enclosure

Charlie licks the frozen blood until his tongue goes tingly. It is not fresh, not warm, or even particularly flavorful. The block melts slowly as he toys with it, but it never heats, never feels alive and flowing.

He waits for the morsels. He licks the red ice and pants, huffing until his whiskers dance.

They arrive all at once, a herd of tall ones and their bite-sized offspring. They swarm the distant railing, and the air fills with the scent of hot dogs.

They lean against the glass wall inside his den, and Charlie wonders if they taste fresh. He watches the little ones move with stuttering steps. They squeal and totter and place filthy hands against the barrier which keeps them alive.

The hot dogs bleed onto their clothing, red ketchup streaks, and dribbles of some sweet drink. The morsels laugh and point while their tall ones snap pictures and Charlie imagines long grass, dry heat, and the rhythm of their steps against baked earth.

He licks the block, grinds a slow divot in the ice, stains his muzzle crimson while they dance outside his prison.

Charlie imagines they would run like gazelle, run in tiny tripping steps. They would scream. They would run. But the morsels would not be fast enough.

They would never be fast enough to live.

Tortoise Enclosure

Oliver's tunnel grows. He has aimed it inward, toward the center of his pen, for he has learned long ago that any outward digging will be quickly backfilled by They-who-bring-food.

To peer into it now would offer a view of a shallow scrape, a domed, tortoise-shaped cross section that angles sharply down but poses no risk of escape.

Oliver has learned.

He has dug his pits through generations of keepers, and so you would have to be a tortoise to fit yourself deep into the hollow at the far back wall and pivot one half turn to the right to realize his digging has continued.

The tunnel moves east, toward the Savannah, angling up again and aiming for all it's worth at the open, grassy picnic square beside the elephant.

He might have less distance to the west, but the macaque's cage has a concrete floor. If he miscalculated there, he could be forced to dig beneath the entire ape house to find freedom.

He will take the slower, safer path. Already, he believes his tunnel has breached the confines of his enclosure. He digs below the zebras now, and if he turns to the left soon, he should emerge amid the picnic tables.

By day, he makes certain to be seen. He trundles, slow as a stone, around the shallow pond, through the tall reeds where Miranda should have lingered. He sleeps in the sun, and when it fades, when They-who-bring-food are gone, Oliver digs.

For freedom. For love. He digs for Miranda.

Zebras

The zebras circle the place where the ground moves. They lower their muzzles to the earth and snort a chorus of echoing rumbles, striped hides heaving all around.

Their leader stamps and the others mimic her.

In the center of their huddle, the packed Savannah lifts and cracks. A bulge appears, rises and falls.

The lead zebra flicks her tail, takes a step backwards, and the ring widens. Voices whisper as the herd digests the anomaly.

"What is it?" "What do we do?"

The ground surges, a boil, a fly bite on the Savannah's skin. It erupts at once, spattering dirt and sending the herd into stumbling flight. They retreat, bolting to the far corner of their fence.

Their hooves beat a fearful dance. They blow and bellow. The leader brays, harsh, screeching.

Nothing horrible happens.

Eventually, they circle back. This time the leader approaches alone. The others murmur encouragement from a safe distance.

Something moves in the broken earth. A blunt head appears, and the herd trembles. A small voice speaks a single, clear-bright word.

"Damn."

The zebras echo him, reverently whisper, "Damn."

The head vanishes. Nothing more emerges and the herd leader gets down to business.

"Hole," she announces. "Hole. There's a hole here. Mind your hooves. Mind your legs."

The herd recovers, taking up the chant and fixing the danger in their memory. "Hole. Mind your hooves. Hole."

Elephant Paddock

Shanti has eaten all her peanuts. Her computations have been erased by The-one-who-sweeps. She stands outside her shelter, in the dark, and tries to count the stars. There are too many lights still on in the zoo, and the heavenly bodies seem to fade in and out, shifting positions as if to spoil her work.

As if taunting her.

She thinks it is unnatural for the night to be so well-lit and swings her trunk in frustration. Shanti rocks on pillar legs and begins again. Six bright stars in a cluster.

She is sorry she ate the peanuts, which were exceptional for counting. For a while she tried to use the straw, but straw is fleeting, too easy to blow aside with even the slightest of sighs.

Shanti swings her trunk. Six stars. She thumps a nearby rock that certainly wasn't there a moment ago.

One rock.

"Hello?

One *tortoise.* He surges forward one short step, and Shanti can see the curve of his shell, the extended neck, and flat-faced head.

"Am I outside the fence?" he asks.

"That depends," Shanti whispers.

"On what?"

"On which fence you mean and which side is outside."

He looks at her for a long time. She can see his two tiny eyes. She can see a pattern of shapes on his shell.

"You're an elephant," he says.

"Yes." Shanti begins to count the shapes.

"Damn." He swivels, shifts so that the patterns move.

"Wait." Shanti imagines she could count them all. If he held still, she could. If he were to follow her into the lighted shelter. The patterns on his shell line up perfectly, orderly, one against the next.

"I'm sorry," he says. "I have to get outside the fence."

"I know how."

Shanti has counted the loose spots, the places she can lift and bend, and he is not nearly as big as an elephant. For a tortoise, there would be more than enough room. If she lifted. If she pried.

If he would only agree to a little bargain.

The Crow

Debra listens to the hyena weep while the sun sets. She perches on the guard rail beside the path, and she tilts her head from one side to the other. When the noises become unbearable, grating, she flies away, circling the cat house and the larger enclosures around it. Tiger. Lion. Bear.

As dark falls, the pathway lights are triggered. She darts between them, an invisible shadow, like death.

Eventually, she settles outside the macaque's cage. He is her favorite victim, but tonight he sulks inside the ape house. His little door is open, but even if he *can* hear her taunts, what fun could she find in them without witnessing his reactions?

Frustrated, she paces the top of the 'Jungle' sign. Every three hops she turns, reverses direction, and changes her view.

Savannah, hop, hop, hop. Jungle, hop hop, hop.

Perhaps she should rejoin the murder, but lately their gossip reeks of repetition. Debra considers inventing something, manufacturing some scandal, but she is a bird of very small imagination.

Just as she decides to relent, however, a sharp creaking drags her back to the Savannah view. Metal complains in the darkness. Something large moves against the linked-chain fence.

Debra bounces once before launching. She flaps. She soars, landing in a tree beside the picnic area. She watches, first with one eye and then the other, as the elephant pries up the bottom of her fence.

The gap the mighty trunk makes is ridiculously small. Not big enough to let its own head escape. But it is not the elephant which squeezes through the opening. It is something low and round. Something that trundles out of the Savannah and steps slowly onto free, green grass.

"Escape." At first Debra whispers. Then, she takes to wing. She circles the darkened cages, circles, and is first to chant it into every ear. "Escape. Escape."

The night rings with her gossip, her triumph.

Escape.

It begins. She feels it like a held breath, like the first pebble forewarning the landslide. Someone is *free*.

Someone is bound to be shot.

Ape House

Gonzo remains inside the house after the rest of his troop emerges. Some days, They-who-bring-food linger in the aisle between the cages. They chatter in their barking voices. Some days they bring the bean with them, and the ape house interior fills with the scent of home.

Gonzo was not born in the house. He remembers a Formosan jungle. He remembers freedom and long afternoons lounging on a branch chewing bean.

Today, the aisle clears quickly, however. He is alone in a world of stone and metal, a concrete maze of parallel bars and tiny square doorways.

His troop is excited about something. Gonzo hears the other male screeching, shaking the rope perches. The females echo him, and a rain of spit seeds and tossed debris patters against the outer wall and floor.

Gonzo rubs his head and face with both paws. He approaches the square door, but does not exit. He listens, and he hears the voice of birds.

"Loose in the zoo."

It is not the rotten crow's voice and carries little of taunt or terror. Gonzo shows the doorway his teeth and ambles into a sunlit morning.

"Someone has escaped!" The youngest female macaque is on him before he takes a step. She lands on top of Gonzo, dropping from the ropes, and just as quickly rolls off.

His head aches. He brushes her off with his paws even though she is already bounding away.

The troop gathers at the front of their territory, where a pair of pigeons strut along the path.

"Turtle," one coos.

The other corrects her. "Tortoise. Free."

Gonzo eyes the sky, the jungle sign, and the rail beside the path. There is no sign of the crow. He drags himself to a far corner, to a place both separate from the troop and near enough to hear the pigeons' chatter.

"Someone is free."

Gonzo's lips stretch. He offers a silent screech, a mute tribute. The-one-who-sweeps approaches, and already he can smell his mistress on the wind.

Hyena Pen

Alice pants atop her stair-step rock. She has spent the morning chasing pigeons, racing from one end of her enclosure to the next, snapping her jaws and snarling at the noisy birds.

They spread lies. Their fat beaks chant of freedom and escape.

Alice hates them.

She will crush their bones if they venture inside the bars. She will chomp and chew while their fat, feathered bodies twitch in her jaws.

Once, when the pups were only just taking their first steps, Alice caught a pigeon unawares. Feigning sleep, she lulled it into a sense of safety, and when it waddled between the bars to search for scraps among her straw, Alice killed and ate it.

The pups were too young then. Too young to learn her trick. What if they are hungry now?

She cackles and glares out through her bars. In the shade of a flowering shrub beside the path, a great stone has appeared. Alice is certain it was not there when she awoke, and she wonders if rocks are born. If they come into the world with pain and panting, or if they simply sprout like the grass and flowers.

She's never seen a new stone before and has always assumed they just *are*. Always there. Always in the same place.

She flicks her tail at a persistent fly and wonders if the rock has a mother. If, somewhere, a larger stone doesn't wonder where this one has gone.

VIDEO FOOTAGE

The video is activated by motion. It streams to the Internet according to a randomized order of camera hierarchy. On the zoo's website, a simple flash player shuffles through cages beneath the boldfaced type reading: ZOO CAM.

Someone's nephew has, upon suggestion, programmed the feed to respond to viewer interest. The more clicks on a particular feed, the more often that camera is displayed. It takes only four hours for the elephant house to dominate the feed. In 24, the recorded highlight video, quickly dubbed, "Asian Elephant Pets Turtle," has gone viral.

On screens all over the world, the elephant traces the multi-faceted shell with her trunk, slowly, methodically. Theories abound as to the nature of the animals' relationship. One commenter remarks that she almost appears to be counting, but they are quickly shot down in favor of more romantic interpretations.

Another points out that the 'turtle' in question is actually a Sulcata tortoise. They are mocked into silence.

When someone questions the presence of a turtle inside the elephant's enclosure, the moderator quickly turns off commenting.

The page views continue to escalate.

Grizzly Grotto

Hector lies on his back with three paws in the air. The fourth cradles half a melon against his chest, saved for a later treat. His head turns to one side so that he may watch the artist as she captures yet another glorious Hector portrait.

All morning long he has been bombarded by birds.

First, the crows came, singing of tragedy. Then the pigeons, clattering and talking over one another. Hector ignores all gossip. He cares little for what happens outside his trench. Inside it, there is only him. Only bear and stump and the attention showered upon him by the artist.

As a cub, Hector was bottle-fed, cradled by They-who-cared, and fawned over almost continuously. When he played with his brother, they would clap and coo. When the cubs wrestled, They-who-cared cheered.

Now his brother is gone. Hector only remembers him as the one who shared this affection. He does not share any longer. Here behind his trench, Hector is the star.

The artist finishes and flips her book around. She shows him her work, always seeks his approval upon finishing.

Hector rolls slowly to a sitting position. He gazes up to the railing, but it is too far. His eyes are not what they once were. Still, he growls agreeably before stuffing the melon half between his jaws. He approves.

The artist claps.

They understand one another. This is the way of things, and Hector likes everything exactly as it is. When another pigeon flutters past the stump, he slaps at it, sends it and its gossip on their way.

He cares nothing for what happens beyond the trench. The bear, the star, is forever on this side of the world.

Lion Enclosure

Charlie hears the birds arguing, but he is too busy rolling in dung to worry. They have brought him a half dozen fresh zebra droppings, and the scent drives him to a frenzy.

His mouth hangs open. He huffs over and over until the odor threatens to overwhelm him. His sides heave. His long tail lashes.

"Escape."

A stupid crow has broken from its flock. It bounces on a nearby stump where the two lionesses that make up Charlie's pride are lounging in the sun.

"Go away." His favorite lioness yawns, showing the bird her teeth in warning.

The crow caws and flaps but remains foolishly in place. Determined. "Someone has escaped."

"Lie," the lioness says.

Beside her, another purrs agreement. It is well known that crows are not to be trusted.

"Someone is out," the bird insists. "They'll be shot for certain."

Charlie huffs and flattens his ears to his skull.

"Who is it?" The female decides to believe the gossip. Her tail-tip, however, twitches, a sure sign she is also considering pouncing on the messenger.

"The tortoise," the crow cackles.

"They'll catch *him* for sure," the lioness says. "But they won't shoot him. They only shoot *fierce* animals." She says it proudly, as if she dares them to try.

Charlie thinks that he is fierce. He thinks the tortoise will be found quickly, but he agrees with the lioness. No one will shoot it.

He has lived at the zoo his whole life, and no one has ever been shot.

The dung bores him now. His head is full of *escape* and *freedom.* There is no room left for odors, however delicious.

At the far end of the enclosure, a crowd has gathered at the railing, at the glass. Charlie heaves himself to his paws and shakes his head, lets his thick mane shiver before stalking toward the gathered morsels.

Tortoise Abroad

Oliver moves in darkness. He has forgotten how cold the world is outside his desert, and how slowly he is forced to move when his limbs are chilled.

When he first emerges from the bushes, a terrible noise assaults him. It takes Oliver two rocking steps to discover the sound is coming from an animal.

There is a barred cage across from his hiding spot. It is raised on a concrete foundation, and there is a fake rock in one corner with many levels. Near the bars, a hyena gapes at him.

Oliver stretches his neck by way of greeting and takes another step.

"Stone," she says. "You are very strange."

"Tortoise," Oliver says. It takes a great deal of his energy to speak.

"No," the hyena laughs. "I'm a hyena."

"Yes." Oliver has lived many lifetimes. He believes a hyena should know a tortoise when she sees one. This one, therefore, has been in a cage her entire life.

He stops moving when he's near enough to look straight up at her.

"Have you seen Miranda?"

"I saw you born," the hyena whispers fiercely. "Do stones have mothers?"

"My mother eats in distant fields," Oliver says. Does she understand? He knows that animals born in the zoo often have unnatural ways of thinking. Is it a waste of his time and energy to linger? He has only a few hours until he must hide again.

"That's sad." The hyena moans and covers her muzzle with both front paws. "I'm sorry."

"I'm looking for a tall bird," Oliver says. Before he can describe his love, the hyena barks an answer.

"Aviary." She surprises him with her confidence. Her head lifts, ears flicking and eyes wide and lucid. "All birds are kept in the aviary."

"Except pigeons," Oliver says.

"And stupid crows." The hyena nods. In this, they fully understand one another.

"But Miranda lives in *my* enclosure," Oliver says. "And she's a bird."

"They were probably just waiting for someone to die," the hyena says.

Oliver thinks she's still talking about crows until she finishes.

"They were just keeping her with you until a cage was free."

Oliver hates this idea, but it is probably correct. He has not planned what to do when he finds Miranda, and he imagines They-who-bring-food simply stealing her away again. He imagines it will be difficult to free her from this aviary. What if the floor, like the hyena's, is thick concrete?

"It's the second path." The hyena's voice brings him back. She is urgent, pressing against the bars and speaking in a squeaking rush. "It's not far. Just take the second path."

"Thank you." He pivots, thinking of bars and concrete.

The hyena watches him go, panting, making sporadic, sharp cackles as he steps. One slow foot after the other. When he is near to the second path, she calls out again.

"That's it. That one there."

Oliver pretends he cannot hear her. He takes the path, though, and her cackles chase him, her final proclamation rings out.

"Very strange stone."

Aviary

The aviary is never silent. Inside its twin pair of double safety doors, hundreds of birds dwell in a state of constant communication.

Sometimes the voices are soft, contemplative. Sometimes they are a trumpet's blast, a declaration of activity and interaction. If the butterfly house is a held breath, the aviary is a conversation, a steady, unrelenting chorus of voices in all registers.

Thousands of plants grow inside. Stout tropical trees, low bushes, and layer upon layer of climbing vine, creeper, palm, fern, and orchid. The air is thick, wet, and aromatic. A false river wanders across the floor beneath the bamboo bridges and the hanging paths. It adds its babble to the cacophony, singing a soft, low, steady baseline to the avian voices.

Above it, hidden among the fronds and branches, birds of every shape and size warble, tweet, caw, and hoot. Tiny, high-pitched voices titter. Large, booming voices honk and squawk.

The flutter of beaks in motion is only matched by the occasional explosion of wings as the flocks of iridescent bodies shift position from one perch to the next.

Every day, the aviary sings non-stop. When one voice pauses, another speaks into the gap. Every breath is sound and secret.

Today, they sing a song of freedom. They sing of liberation and escape. Outside their walls they hear the lesser birds' gossip. Inside, they make of it a cantata, an aria, a symphony of excitement.

Escape is not unknown here, despite the signs on all the double doors that read: Please Close Outside Door Before Opening Interior Door. They-who-open-doors do not follow rules, and someone leaves from time to time.

The aviary sings of their foolishness for days afterward.

It is cold outside. It is often dry and dark and unforgiving.

"Escape," the aviary sings. "Escape. The last desperate act of fools."

See part I of Frances Pauli's story "The Zoo Diaries" online at Metaphorosis.
If you liked it, leave a comment. Authors love that!
Remember to subscribe to our e-mail updates so you'll know when new stories are posted.

About the story

"The Zoo Diaries" came about as the result of a challenge given me by a dear author friend. He suggested we spend a full year waking up each morning and writing by hand, a single, self-contained entry of micro fiction that would string together over the months into a cohesive story. Despite the fact that I am not a morning person, and the idea of an even earlier start caused me to break out in hives, I accepted the challenge based on two things. First, I had (and alas, still do) a surplus of lovely blank journals which were simply begging to be written in by hand. Second, I trusted the wisdom of this particular author friend and wanted to see how my prose shifted and deepened when I took the time to write long form. The idea for "The Zoo Diaries" came to me when I was searching for a concept that could be told in an episodic fashion, in short bursts each morning. I decided to tell the story of a zoo and its inmates, but to pass that story from one cage to the other each day, in the fashion of gossip whispered from one animal to the next so that the tale might travel even though its tellers were not allowed that freedom.

A question for the author

Q: What's easier for you - imagining a happier world, or a darker one?

A: I'm not sure it's easier, but I do my best to imagine a happier world, to focus my energies on how we can improve life on this planet rather than to give energy to the ways in which we might sink deeper into darkness. Imagination has power, and I believe in focusing that toward the goal of a brighter future, to inspire myself to act in ways that can contribute to that potential.

About the author

Frances Pauli lives in Washington state with her family, a small menagerie, and far too many houseplants. She enjoys a plant-based, vegan lifestyle, animal activism, and of course, reading. She writes stories about animal characters, often in the speculative fiction category.

francespauli.com, @mothindarkness

Copyright

Title information

Metaphorosis January 2023

ISSN: 2573-136X (online)
ISBN: 978-1-64076-249-7 (e-book)
ISBN: 978-1-64076-250-3 (paperback)

Publisher

Metaphorosis

a magazine of speculative fiction

Metaphorosis Magazine is an imprint of Metaphorosis Publishing
Neskowin, OR, USA

www.metaphorosis.com

"Metaphorosis" is a registered trademark.

Discounts available

Substantial discounts are available for educational institutions, including writing workshops. Discounts are also available for quantity purchases. For details, contact Metaphorosis at metaphorosis.com/about

Metaphorosis Publishing

Metaphorosis offers beautifully written science fiction and fantasy. Our imprints include:

Metaphorosis Magazine
Plant Based Press
Verdage
Vestige

You can also find us:
@MetaphorosisMag, @Metaphorosis
www.facebook.com/metaphorosis

Help keep Metaphorosis running by supporting us at
Patreon.com/metaphorosis

See more about some of our books on the following pages.

Metaphorosis Magazine

Metaphorosis
a magazine of speculative fiction

Metaphorosis is an online speculative fiction magazine dedicated to quality writing. We publish an original story every week, along with author bios, interviews, and notes on story origins.

We also publish monthly print and e-book issues, as well as yearly Best of and Complete anthologies.

Come and see us online at magazine.Metaphorosis.com.

Metaphorosis
2021
Metaphorosis
Best of 2020
Metaphorosis
2020
Metaphorosis
Best of 2019
Metaphorosis
2019
Metaphorosis
Best of 2018
Metaphorosis
2018
Metaphorosis
Best of 2017
Metaphorosis
2017

Metaphorosis
Best of 2016

Metaphorosis
2016
Editor
B. Morris Allen

Plant Based Press

Vegan-friendly science fiction and fantasy, including anthologies of the year's best SFF stories, from 2016-2020.

Chambers of the Heart

speculative stories
by
B. Morris Allen

A heart that's a building, a dog that's a program, a woman sinking irretrievably — stories about love, loss, and movement.

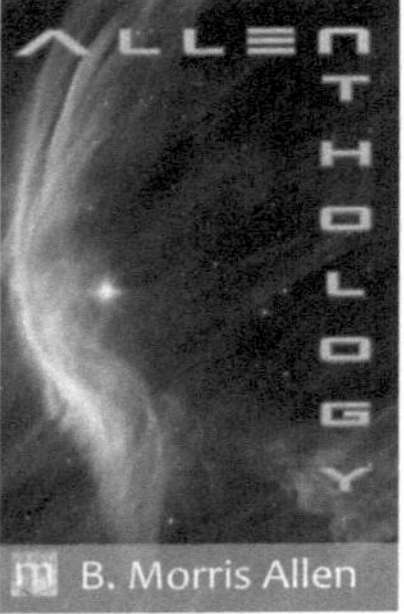

Susurrus

A darkly romantic story of magic, love, and suffering.

Allenthology: Volume I

Including three full collections of SFF stories.

Verdage

Science fiction and fantasy books for writers — full of great stories, often with an additional focus on the craft of speculative fiction writing.

Reading 5X5 x3

Changes

How do stories move from 'maybe' to published?

Here are 15 case studies of stories published in *Metaphorosis* magazine.

Reading 5X5 x2

Duets

How do authors' voices change when they collaborate?

A round-robin of five talented science fiction and fantasy authors collaborating with each other and writing solo.

Including stories by Evan Marcroft, David Gallay, J. Tynan Burke, L'Erin Ogle, and Douglas Anstruther.

Score

an SFF symphony

An anthology with an emotional score from the heights of joy to the depths of despair – but always with a little hope shining through.

Reading 5X5

Five stories, five times

See how different
writers take on
the same material.

Reading 5X5

Writers' Edition

Two extra stories,
the story seed,
and authors' notes
on writing.

Vestige

Novelettes, novellas, and novels by Metaphorosis authors.

The Nocturnals
Mariah Montoya

Night is Dangerous.
Day is deadly.

Where day and night last thirty years, humans move constantly stay ahead of the night and cruel Nocturnals that call it home. But a boy is lost out there.